For Don Watson

in memory of Fay

First published 2009 by
FREMANTLE PRESS
25 Quarry Street, Fremantle
(PO Box 158, North Fremantle 6159)
Western Australia
www.fremantlepress.com.au

Copyright text © Dianne Wolfer, 2009.
Copyright illustrations
© Brian Simmonds 2009.

Cover and digital collages
designed by Tracey Gibbs.

Printed by Everbest
Printing Company, China.

National Library of Australia
Cataloguing-in-publication data

Wolfer, Dianne, 1961-

Lighthouse girl / Dianne Wolfer;
illustrator, Brian Simmonds.

2nd Ed.

ISBN: 978 1921 696 57 2

Lighthouses — Juvenile fiction.
World War, 1914–1918 —
Juvenile fiction.

A823.3

Publication of this title was assisted
by the Commonwealth Government
through the Australia Council, its arts
funding and advisory body.

Lighthouse Girl

Dianne Wolfer

illustrated by Brian Simmonds

'*Happy* Birthday.'

Fay's father handed her a package wrapped in brown paper.

'What is it?'

'Open it and see.'

Fay Catherine Howe untied the string and flipped through a book of empty pages.

'It's a journal,' her father said. 'I'm worried about you living out here on Breaksea Island with just two old lighthouse keepers for company. Keeping a diary might be like having a friend to talk to.'

'But I have Jacko,' Fay replied.

'A donkey isn't what I had in mind,' Father laughed.

'He's a good listener!'

'He is that.'

August 5ᵗʰ 1914

I love my new diary, especially its soft red cover. I'm going to write down all my plans for the future. But those plans might have to change. Father received a telegraph. Britain has declared war on Germany – on my birthday!

Prime Minister Cook said, 'When the Empire is at war, so also is Australia.'

Father and Joe were talking about the German leader, Kaiser Wilhelm II. He's invaded Belgium and Belgium is our ally, that's why we have to help. Joe also said something about Archduke Franz Ferdinand. I'm not sure who he is. It was too windy to hear properly.

I wonder if war will change things for us here on Breaksea?

The War!

Us

Kaiser Wilhelm II

King George V

MESSAGE FROM THE KING

The Prime Minister (Mr. Cook) on Wednesday officially announced an outbreak of war between England and Germany. He added: "Australia is now at war."

From His Majesty the King the following message has been received by the Governor-General, through the Secretary of State for the Colonies:– "I desire to express to my people of the overseas dominions the appreciation and pride with which I have received the messages from their respective Governments during the last few days. These spontaneous assurances of their fullest support recall to me the generous self-sacrificing help given by them in the past to the mother country. I shall be strengthened in the discharge of the great responsibilities which rest upon me by the confident belief that in this time of trial my Empire will stand united, calm and resolute and trusting in God."

Mr Cook
– he has a kind face, I think.

Some days Fay wrote about life on the island.
Other days she wrote about the world beyond Breaksea.
Sometimes she wrote a mixture of the two.

August 10th

I'm sheltering in Lizard Cave – out of the roaring wind. The sea's too rough for Stan's supply boat, so we're living off rabbit and nettles. Again! When the rain stops, I'll go out with the rifle. We're desperate for meat. In the meantime, I'm snug and warm. This cave is my favourite place. I can hear mutton-bird chicks peeping in their burrows while seals play on the rocks below. The war seems so far away ...

August 11th

Young men are lining up at the recruiting centres. They can't wait to fight the Kaiser. Father says the government is gathering a mighty fleet to take them to Europe. I wonder if Harold will enlist? I can't imagine my brother as a soldier.

August 17th

On Sunday night there were 1500 people at the railway station to farewell the Albany recruits. A local nurse has signed up, too.

The Albany Brass Band gave the soldiers a rousing send-off. Joe reckoned he could hear them playing 'The Girl I Left Behind' from the lighthouse balcony. I couldn't hear anything above the racket of the petrels. They were cooing and calling from their burrows until dawn.

THE COMMONWEALTH

AUSTRALIAN-IMPERIAL EXPEDITIONARY FORCE

ALBANY'S CONTRIBUTION

SEND-OFF TO THE MEN ON SUNDAY

Albany's contribution to the West Australian contingent of the Australian-Imperial Expeditionary Force left by the train on Sunday night for Perth, and the departure of the men was made the occasion of a great popular demonstration at the railway station. It was only in the afternoon that the 30 men were chosen. Up to Saturday just over 100 applications had been received locally but others were expected from the country. The ranks could not thus be closed until Sunday. By the train then ten men arrived and they hastened to the drill hall to undergo medical examination by Dr. Blackburne. Some of these were unaware they would be selected when they left home in the morning but on being passed they accepted the condition imposed and left at night, with the other volunteers for Perth, employment and private considerations apparently being set aside utterly. The chosen few marched from the drill hall to catch the train preceded by the Albany Brass Band. A large crowd followed them through the streets and at the railway station fully 1,500 people assembled. The men pulled up in the station yard, where they were addressed at length by the Mayor. He talked a lot about going to

the front and the Empire, and enjoined them to behave themselves. The crowd chafed at the delay and kept moving forward. Ultimately the men marched on the platform and entrained. Sergt-Major Smith went up with them, as also did Lieut. Riley. Before the train left the band played "The Red, White and Blue", "Auld Lang Syne" and "The Girl I Left Behind Me" and the train departed amidst the most enthusiastic cheering. The following are the names of the 30 chosen men:—

August 21st

Last night I had strange dreams – German soldiers in pointy helmets were rowing across to Breaksea, but Jacko wouldn't let them land. He kept kicking the soldiers into the sea as they tried to climb onto the jetty. I wasn't the only one who had a restless night. This morning Father was tired and grumpy. I think he's worried that Harold will sign up. I'll make some bread and butter pudding to cheer him up.

Winter waves crashed. The wind howled.
Every night Breaksea Lighthouse blinked its steady
warning. Every day Fay wrote in her diary.

August 24th

Another cold front with gales and high seas. The window panes are crusty with salt. It blows into everything.

Father is tending the light while Joe mans the telegraph line. They say there's a ship beyond the Sound. I wouldn't want to be out there tonight.

August 25th

I'm cosy by the fire, cooking mutton-bird stew. I can't make it taste the way Mother used to – mine's too greasy – but it's a change from rabbit.

August 26th

Rain. Again!

And sheets of lightning.

Another day of stew and nettles. The stew is thin. We need flour to thicken it, but we've run out. I hope Stan's supply boat can get across tomorrow.

The cold wind cuts through my shawl and blisters my lips. On days like this, I wish we lived on the mainland.

Albany
×

Michaelmas Island

King George Sound

Breaksea Island

*F*ay cleaned the rifle and hung two mutton-birds in the coolroom ready to pluck. She took the bedding into the sunshine, then ran to the lookout with her pencils and journal. The whales were back.

August 26th

There's a pod of humpbacks breaching near Bald Head – four adults and a calf. I love drawing their tails, but I can't get the rest of their bodies right. It would be easier if they swam closer, but then the whalers might see them …

August 29th

The little penguins are so brave. They jump out of the sea onto the slippery rocks – even in the wildest weather! Then, when they've found their land legs, they waddle home, quick as they can, to their burrows.

Now that breeding season has started, every shrub and rocky overhang seems to hide a growing penguin family.

In mid-September the winter winds eased and the Leeuwin Current began weakening.

September 13th

The supply boat is crossing the harbour — finally!

And Father is calling. He needs Jacko and I'm the only one who can catch him. Poor Jacko. He hates trudging up the steep track weighed down with supplies.

Midday

Fresh meat — hurrah! With flour, eggs, butter, carrots, plenty of potatoes and even a few apples. Stan also brought me two new ribbons — lovely pale green ones!— and copies of the Albany Advertiser, so now we can catch up on the news.

I love supply boat days!

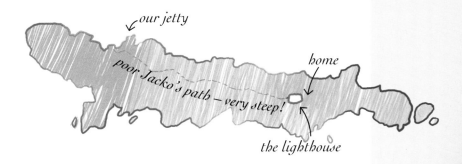

our jetty

poor Jacko's path — very steep!

home

the lighthouse

Fay could taste spring in the sou'westerlies swirling over the sea foam. She wandered down to the sheltered cove where no one could see her, then rolled down her stockings and dipped her toes into the ocean. The water was icy.

September 21ˢᵗ

It's Jacko's birthday.

I'm not sure how old he is. Jacko was on Breaksea long before our family came. He loves spring, so each year I celebrate his birthday in September.

This morning I made him a crown of daisies, but he keeps shaking it off.

Happy birthday Jacko!

One morning Fay's father received an urgent message. Troopships, packed with soldiers from eastern Australia and New Zealand, were steaming towards King George Sound.

'They're on their way to the war,' Father said, 'and they'll be stopping in Albany to take on coal and water. We'll see them as they pass Breaksea.'

Fay gazed out to sea. 'I'll be able to take Jacko to the edge of the cliff and wave to all the soldiers!'

'That you will,' her father laughed.

October 24th

The first troopships have arrived. They're enormous. Clouds of smoke gush from their funnels and bright flags billow from their forestays. The wind is wild, but these ships weather the gales like ducks on a pond.

We're so proud of our men, answering the call to defend the Mother Country. I waved to the soldiers. Some waved back!

October 25th

More ships have arrived. The wind is still blowing a gale, and the harbour hums with the drone of massive steam engines. Smaller boats are scooting back and forth provisioning the ships with coal, water and food. Father has lent me his binoculars. From the lighthouse balcony, I can see people gathering on Mount Clarence to watch. Lucky us. We have the best view in town.

Later

HMAS Melbourne is cruising to and fro behind Breaksea, guarding the fleet. Father says a German raiding ship is prowling along the coast, but seeing the Melbourne makes me feel safe. I'm sure the Germans would think twice before tackling her!

October 26th

Another stormy day.

There are twenty-eight Australian ships and ten from New Zealand anchored in the Sound. What a fleet!

The ships are taking turns to dock at the Deepwater Jetty. Father says Albany has never seen anything like this …

*S*tan delivered fresh supplies and told Fay the troops were going to march along York Street.

'Father,' Fay called. 'The soldiers are marching in Albany. Can I go across to cheer them on?'

'With 30,000 men in town, I don't think so!'

'I could stay with Evelyn.'

'Your sister will be busy with the baby.'

'But Father …'

He shook his head. 'You're needed here.'

'But Stan said they have mascots. I'd love to see them …'

The lighthouse keeper frowned and Fay knew he wouldn't budge.

It's so unfair, she thought, I'm almost grown up. Old enough to go ashore without him!

October 27th

FATHER IS SO MEAN!

or Keeling Island.

THE COMMONWEALTH

Australian Help

THE COMMONWEALTH & NEW
ZEALAND CONTINGENTS.

DEPARTURE FROM ALBANY

From the first, numbers of troops were landed in detachments for marching exercise, as many as 1,500 coming ashore at one time. With the men came bands and regimental mascots in the form of all conceivable breeds of dogs, and in some instances a march of ten miles was made. There was a little leave, but not much, and really only officers and men with business to transact spent any time in the town. Night and day the scene was one pulsating with life. Signalling was constantly kept up, and the military and naval authorities ashore worked at fever-heat day in, day out, meeting calls made on them by the fleet.

Look what I missed out on.

*F*ay stood beside the lighthouse staring at the fleet. The nearest troopship was anchored just half a nautical mile from the island. She lifted her father's binoculars and watched the men going about their jobs. Suddenly Fay blinked in surprise. Two soldiers were waving.

Fay looked around. She and Jacko were the only ones in sight. She waved back.

The soldiers waved again. One soldier unfurled red and yellow semaphore flags. He stretched his right arm and held his left arm low. 'H,' Fay thought. Then the soldier raised his left arm and dropped his right to make an 'E'. He followed with two 'L's and an 'O'.

Fay laughed and hurried inside to get her own flags. She had been signalling ships most of her life and was an expert in semaphore.

October 28th

I've been flag-chatting with the soldiers all afternoon. They're tired of being cooped up on their ship. They can't wait to reach Europe and get into the action. Some of them are homesick. They've asked me to telegraph their families to let them know they're all right. I've written down their messages.

SEMAPHORIC ALPHABET

A

'What are the soldiers saying?' Fay's father asked.

'They're telling me about the voyage and where they're from. They want us to telegraph their families.'

Her father laughed. 'And when would I find time to do that! Joe and I have been working all hours since the fleet arrived.'

'I could do it,' Fay said, showing Father one of the messages.

Dearest Kate
We've arrived safely into Albany's King George Sound.
Not an hour passes without me thinking
about you and the twins. I hope your
cough is better. Save your strength my
dearest, and don't worry about me.
I will take all care. Your Andrew

Father's face grew pale. Fay guessed he was thinking about her mother who'd died just seven months earlier.

'I need to get back to work,' the lighthouse keeper whispered, 'but if you want to send their messages, then you have my permission.'

He smiled sadly and his weather-worn hands ruffled his daughter's hair. 'Go on then girl, be off with you!'

October 28th 5.00pm

My dots and dashes of love, hope and sorrow are travelling across Australia on the telegraph line.

I've been tapping all afternoon, and tomorrow the soldiers' families will receive good news from their boys.

I feel so proud that even out here on Breaksea, I can help the war effort in my own small way.

A	· —	N	— ·
B	— · · ·	O	— — —
C	— · — ·	P	· — — ·
D	— · ·	Q	— — · —
E	·	R	· — ·
F	· · — ·	S	· · ·
G	— — ·	T	—
H	· · · ·	U	· · —
I	· ·	V	· · · —
J	· — — —	W	· — —
K	— · —	X	— · · —
L	· — · ·	Y	— · — —
M	— —	Z	— — · ·

Some of our brave men.

$\mathcal{B}$efore the sun disappeared into the ocean, Fay took her flags outside again. She wanted to let the soldiers know that their messages were on the way. As she watched stars appear in the dusky sky, Fay imagined the faces of the wives and mothers receiving their telegrams.

October 28th 9.00pm

It's late and my wrist aches, but I don't mind. I'm happy to be able to help Our Brave Boys. Some of the messages made me blush. Others made me cry. One was very special. I'm not sure what to make of it …

My name is Charlie. They say you're sending messages to loved ones. I don't have any loved ones. Can I send a message to you?

Yes.

What is your name?

Fay.

That is a pretty name. Are you pretty?

I didn't know what to reply!

I bet you are. What colour are your eyes?

Green.

My favourite colour! Mine are hazel. I'll send you a postcard when we get there. Wish me luck.

Good luck, Charlie. Godspeed. Return safely.

*F*ay stared at Charlie's ship, then gazed up at Venus pinpricking the darkening sky. Petrels swooped around her, before crash-landing by their burrows after a day of fishing.

October 29th

Last night I lay awake thinking of Mother. I remember how the two of us patched clothes and baked together in the kitchen after Ada died. I remember the smell of her handkerchiefs and the way she tied her apron. Best of all, I remember how she taught me to read the stars — long before she taught me to read books. But now something terrible is happening.

I'm ashamed even to write it …

I think I'm forgetting her face. I keep trying to picture her eyes but they've become hazy.

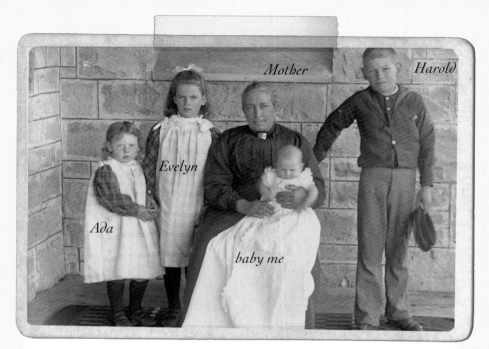

Ada

Evelyn

Mother

Harold

baby me

getting bigger

'Wake up,' Fay's father called. 'The wind's shifted and those cinematographers will be here by midday.'

Fay flung off her blankets. They hardly ever had visitors. She needed to sweep the cottage and air the bedding. And what on earth could she give their guests for lunch?

October 30th 11.00am

The cottage is sparkling. I've collected flowers and set out the best china, just like Mother would have. I tried to remember how she used to arrange things. I hope I've done everything right.

Stan's boat is crossing the Sound. Time to put my scones into the oven.

The harbour is so full. There are thirty-six troopships at anchor!

October 30th 3.00pm

The cinematographers brought fresh eggs, cream and strawberries. What a treat! We haven't had strawberries since last summer.

I put the cream into a china pot beside the jam and we had a proper afternoon tea. It was such fun.

The fleet leaves tomorrow morning at first light. The cinematographers will film the troopships as they sail off to the war. Today they let me look through their lenses and I filmed Father walking to the lighthouse.

*H*MS *Minotaur* raised anchor at dawn. She steamed out of King George Sound flanked by HMAS *Sydney*. The troopships followed.

Fay watched the *Orvieto* lead the first column of Australian ships. *Wiltshire* led the second line. Then came *Euripides* at the head of the third division. The New Zealanders brought up the rear. Fishing boats and whalers tooted their goodbyes while the naval foghorns boomed a defiant reply.

The ships sailed so close to Breaksea that Fay could see their names glinting in the sunlight: *Tahiti, Limerick, Star of India*. The cinematographers' cameras whirred while Fay waved and waved.

November 1st

Look out Kaiser Wilhelm – the Australian Imperial Expeditionary Force is on its way!

It's taken nearly three hours for the ships to clear the Sound. The convoy waited behind Breaksea until the last New Zealand troopship passed. Then they fell into sailing formation and steamed westwards. Father said the fleet stretches across seven nautical miles! King George must be heartened to know our soldiers are coming to help.

The cinematographers say their footage will be excellent.

Our guests have eaten so much, I had to give them cold cuts and leftover scones for lunch. I could have made rabbit stew, but didn't think it would be ladylike to go out with the gun.

HMS Minotaur
HMAS Sydney
Orvieto
Wiltshire
Euripides
Tahiti
Limerick
Star of India
Waimana
Hymettus
Suffolk
Katuna
Benalla
Southern
Geelong
Port Lincol
Ibut

After the cinematographers left, Fay abandoned her chores to sit with Jacko on her favourite rocky knoll. She imagined the soldiers sailing westwards, surrounded by the vast ocean. Albany would be their last glimpse of Australian soil.

As Fay watched storm clouds gathering on the horizon, she wondered how many of the waving soldiers would return.

November 5th

Life has settled back into the old routine of cooking, cleaning, darning socks and shooting rabbits …

November 10th

Out of supplies. Again!

November 11th

Joe's just heard some exciting news …

HMAS Sydney hit the Emden, that German raider that's been prowling along the coast. She sank off the Cocos Islands. Hurrah. That's one less enemy ship to worry about!

At Sea

THE EMDEN SUNK

WORK OF H.M.A.S. SYDNEY.

Perth, Tuesday.

Yesterday morning the Emden put in an appearance off Cocos Island. The cable officials saw her coming and flashed the news through both ways. She was evidently about to make an attack. After that the cable was silent and the presumption is that the cruiser made quick despatch of the station and its line of communication. After wrecking the station she came into contact with the Australian cruiser Sydney. A running fight of 16 miles ensued and the Sydney sank the Emden off Cocos or Keeling Island.

November 21st

A tiny seahorse washed up under the jetty. I found it while I was waiting for Stan.

The Albany Advertiser finally reported the Great Convoy's visit to Albany. Stan said there's been a news blackout because of the Emden, but now it's safe to let everyone know about our fleet. Suddenly the war doesn't seem so far away.

attached by a strong naval escort

In no other port of the Commonwealth were the ships seen together. The vessels making up the fleet presented an aggregate tonnage of 300,000 tons and on board was an army approaching 30,000 men, with full fighting equipment. Such was the armada that passed the night of October 31 in King George Sound and which put to sea at daylight next morning under the escort of six of the most formidable warships of the age. Such a sight has certainly never been seen before in Australasia, and no man or woman breathing today will probably live to witness another spectacle in any way approaching it in magnificence.

* * * *

It is possibly the nature of man to value

←

Well I was certainly impressed by the fleet's magnificence! Father grinned as he read the article. He says we had a ringside seat in history.

Fay lazed on the jetty reading her diary. The swell tossed fingerlings around the wooden pylons below her. The tiny fish twirled towards the granite boulders then darted back to safer waters. As Fay watched them struggle, she wondered what Charlie and his mates were doing.

December 3rd

No news yet of the Australian soldiers. I sent Charlie a Christmas letter. I hope he won't think I'm being forward, writing before he does.

December 8th

Father heard that bottles with messages from the soldiers are washing ashore at Ellen Cove. I wonder whether Charlie tossed a bottle overboard?

December 15th

The Country Women's Association has sent over a huge bag of wool. They want me to knit scarves for the men at the front. I know it's my duty, but knitting makes me sad. It reminds me of Mother and how we used to do handiwork together.

I think I'll try knitting socks, too. I haven't learnt to do heels properly – Mother ran out of time to teach me – but if they're warm, the soldiers might not mind socks with odd heels.

THE EXPEDITIONARY FORCE

There were those intimately associated with the Australian and New Zealand Expeditionary forces, which left Albany on November 1, who said the majority of the men were homesick. It is no discredit to a man under such circumstances, and the statement seemed to possess little importance at the time. Since the departure of the transports, however, discoveries have been made which recall the remark and emphasise the truth of it. That many minds turned to the homes left behind is proved by the number of messages to friends that were enclosed in bottles and thrown overboard at sea, to be subsequently found washed up on the sea beaches in this vicinity. Bottles of all descriptions — lollie bottles, mineral water bottles and even beer bottles — were used as envelopes and the messages were written on all conceivable odds and ends of paper. In some instances several men shared the same fragment and the tenor of most inscriptions — in the main they were but inscriptions — read:– "Will the finder kindly communicate with so and so — all well". Hundreds of such bottles were found round the enclosing shores of the harbour, on Middleton Beach and on the beaches further east as far as Two-People Bay, 25 miles away. Some were, of course, thrown into the water while the ships lay at anchor but others were evidently committed to the tender care of the ocean far way from land. All conveyed a reminder to absent friends, some messages being more sentimental than others. Very many of these extraordinary messages have reached this office. The 30 000 men now in Egypt must have left many friends behind and it is particularly fitting at this season of the year to recall the fact that the thoughts of those departing were with them when the time came to take leave of Australia.

Brass Band. A l

$\mathcal{F}$ay hummed carols as she waited for Stan. He'd promised to bring extra rations for Christmas.

'I have something special from Evelyn,' Stan called as he dropped anchor beside the jetty.

'What is it?'

'A plum pudding.'

Fay grinned. As she sniffed the pudding Jacko brayed loudly at the sight of so many boxes.

December 21ˢᵗ

Evelyn's plum pudding smells delicious! Stan also brought fresh vegetables and the latest Albany Advertiser. Our war correspondent says Australian soldiers are training near Cairo in Egypt.

Australian Imperial Expeditionary Force

CAMP IN THE DESERT

FIRST OFFICIAL PRESS REPORT

Melbourne, Tuesday.

The following cable message from Mr. Charles Bean, the Commonwealth war correspondent with the Australian-Imperial Expeditionary force and dated Cairo yesterday, was received today:– "The regular training of the Australian force began today. Looking from the Pyramids, the desert northwards appeared to be studded with bodies of troops moving in every direction. Each unit has its allotted portion of the desert and marches there in the morning. The training goes on almost continuously till sundown. Practically the whole of the force is now in camp on the desert, either at the Pyramids or at Maadi, across the Nile. Camp streets have been outlined with stones brought from dumps at the scene of excavations in an ancient Egyptian cemetery on the hill above the camp. The new street is now well lighted with incandescent and electric lights. Trams are running into the heart of the camp. This particular street shows one constant procession of camels and donkeys, both often carrying a soldier and a native. Lorries drawn by mules also make endless strings. The horses are getting used to the camels but the sight of a single soldier trying to induce four Australian draught horses to pass a camel or donkey without pulling the groom to pieces in the process, is still worth seeing."

Imagine spending Christmas at the Pyramids. If I were a young man, I'd join up tomorrow!

The lighthouse keepers celebrated Christmas with roast chicken, baked vegetables and plum pudding. Fay made paper chains from old newspapers and followed her mother's recipe for creamy custard. The weather was clear and no ships interrupted their celebrations.

December 25th

Father gave me buttons and lace for my sewing box. I gave him a pair of socks (with strange heels). There's so much wool, I don't think the CWA ladies will mind. I've already knitted five scarves to send to the front.

Joe gave me three new pencils. They're Derwents! Pale blue, red and that bright green I've always wanted.

'For drawing in your journal,' Joe said.

I gave him a card with a sketch of HMAS Sydney. He told me I should become an artist!

It's been a quiet Christmas. I wish Harold and my sisters were here. Father said Grace and a Christmas prayer but I knew his heart wasn't in it. And the custard was lumpy. I can't make it smooth the way Mother used to.

CHRISTMAS GREETINGS

GOD DEFEND THE RIGHT

On New Year's Eve Fay sat up late, watching the Albany lights flicker on the water.

Moonlight traced pale ribbons over the still harbour as the shearwaters screeched a noisy welcome to 1915.

A few days later, Stan brought the New Year edition of the *Albany Advertiser*. It mentioned the troops again, but there was still no postcard from Charlie.

1915!

THE COMMONWEALTH

THE EXPEDITIONARY FORCES.

London,   Tuesday.
The men of the Australian and New
Zealand contingents are undergoing heavy
work to fit them for the field in their camp in
the desert outside Cairo. All are in the best
of spirits and anxious to get fighting. Their
fine physique and the excellence of their
horses are attracting favourable attention.

January 14th

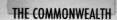

*Stan brought mail with the supplies. There are four postcards
from Egypt – from soldiers I don't even know!*

*The soldiers wrote to thank me for telegraphing messages to
their loved ones. They've addressed the postcards to 'The Little
Girl on Breaksea Island, Albany, Western Australia'.*

*Since they left, I've grown another inch, so I'm not really a
<u>little</u> girl any more … The sun must have been in their eyes!*

A View from the Hospital, of the Harbour with Warships & Transports in the Bay. Looking West

WAY OUT TO SEA.

OUR HOSPITAL TENTS

Have 50/A Here

AUSTRALIAN REST CAMP.

ΑΓΓΛΟΓΑΛΛΙΚΟΣ ΣΤΟ...
FLOTTE ANGLO-FRANCAISE ~ MOUDROS TH...

NOTHING is to be written on this side except the date and signature of the sender. Sentences not required may be erased. If anything else is added the post card will be destroyed.

I am quite well.

I have been admitted into hospital

{ sick } and am going on well.
{ wounded } and hope to be discharged soon.

I am being sent down to the base.

I have received your { letter dated 14/11/16
{ telegram „ _____
{ parcel „ _____

Letter follows at first opportunity.

I have received no letter from you
{ lately.
{ for a long time.

Signature } *J. G. List*
only.

Date _____ /14

[Postage must be prepaid on any letter or post card addressed to the sender of this card.]

(83509) Wt. W3497-293 2,250m. 4/16 J. J. K. & Co., Ltd.

The Empire Theatre in Albany was screening the cinematographers' film of the Expeditionary Force sailing past Breaksea. Joe offered to do a double shift so that Fay's father could take her over to the mainland.

'Do you think we'll be in the film?' Fay asked.

'Of course not,' he replied.

'We might be …'

Fay tried on her dresses, but neither of them felt right for such a special occasion.

'They're too short!'

'You've grown,' her father said. 'Evelyn will have to take you shopping before the screening.'

Fay had never bought a new dress. Her mother had sewn all her clothes. Fay was so excited she could hardly sleep. As she tossed and turned she heard the wind shift. She peered out her window and saw clouds skidding over the moon.

'Go away,' Fay whispered to the clouds.

They didn't listen.

January 24th

*The weather has turned and the island is shrouded in mist.
We have disappeared. It's unfair. I haven't been to town for so
long. Evelyn's baby will be all grown by the time I'm able to
get off this stupid island!*

January 25th

Still foggy.

*Only the lighthouse is visible.
We're like castaways cut off from
the rest of the world.*

*And we missed both screenings of
The Departure.*

EMPIRE THEATRE
YORK STREET, ALBANY

Theatre Phone 132 - Residence 132 - Reservations at Berryman's

EMPIRE THEATRE.

Direction Empire Picture Co.   Manager, F. Clarke-Cottrell

To-night and Monday Night !

STILL ON TOP !   PROGRAMME DE LUXE !
——"It's a Long Way to Tipperary"——

COME AND SEE

The Australian Armada in King George's

THE DEPARTURE ON
NOVEMBER 1   **Sound.**   THE DEPARTURE ON
NOVEMBER 1

MY FRIEND FROM INDIA—Edison Comedy, in three parts
RECREATION—A Keystone—Charles Chaplin Scream
PATHE WAR GAZETTE—All the Latest
DOLLY OF THE DAILIES—Thrilling ! Thrilling !
AMONG THE CLOUDS—the Building of a Skyscraper
WITH THE WARRIORS AT YPRES—the Latest

Patriotic Songs by Percy Coward !   A Brilliant Programme !

BRIGHT MUSIC.   -   POPULAR PRICES—2s and 1s

Booking Free—Ring 103.   Field's Tea Rooms, Empire Buildings.

AFTER
CHURCH | **SUNDAY NIGHT** | AFTER
CHURCH
——EMPIRE THEATRE——

Grand Picture Entertainment

(By permission of the Hon. the Colonial Secretary) an approved Programme
——will be presented in aid of——

Patriotic and Local Charity Fund.

*W*hile Fay waited for Stan, she sketched an unusual rock above the jetty. The rock had an uncanny, ancient feeling to it. It was shaped like an elephant – not a cheerful circus beast, but a strange, brooding creature. Whenever Fay was alone, she felt it watching her. Fay shivered, glad to see Stan's boat passing Whaling Cove. A brisk westerly plumped his sails. She knew he'd soon reach Breaksea.

'Mail for you,' Stan called as he threw the mooring ropes, 'from a young Charlie.'

So much for privacy, Fay thought. She tucked the postcard into her pocket and hurried Jacko up the hill. Fay wanted to be alone when she read the postcard.

POST CARD

PLACE
POSTAGE

STAMP
HERE

DEC 22 1914

FIELD POST

Dear Green Eyes

We've landed in Egypt. You should see the pyramids — they're enormous — much bigger than they look on this card! And guess what? Our unit organised a camel race. I'm the youngest, so they made me jockey. Camels aren't easy to ride — and they're grumpy beggars — but I managed to stay on and we won. It was such a lark. And it meant extra rations, so boy am I popular today!

I hope you will write to me.

Charlie

Fay of the Green Eyes
Breaksea Island, near Albany, Western Australia

'Fay, where are you? Why aren't you helping Stan with the supplies? And why hasn't poor Jacko been rubbed down?'

'I'm coming …'

'Stan said you received another postcard,' her father continued. 'From some Charlie fellow.'

Fay nodded, glaring at Stan as she handed over her postcard.

'How does this Charlie know you have green eyes?' Father demanded.

'He asked me!'

Before the lighthouse keeper could say any more, Fay scribbled a reply. She knew she'd have to be quick. Stan was waiting to catch the tide.

> *Dear Charlie*
> *Thank you for your card.*
> *Did you really ride a camel?*
> *All is fine here. The mutton-bird chicks are hatching. And Jacko is well.*
> *You're in my prayers each night.*
> *Take care.*
> *Fay*

She tossed her plaits as she handed the sealed letter to Stan. I'm old enough to send private letters, she thought crossly. Her father raised his eyebrows but didn't say anything. Stan grinned as Fay turned back to her chores.

February 28th

Stan brought another message from Charlie. Our mail must have crossed over. I wonder what the field censor blocked out?

POST · CARD

Dear Fay

You sent me a letter. My first ever. Thank you!

It was a strange Christmas and New Year.

██████████████████████████ We're all training hard.

Thanks for writing. It meant a lot to me.

Will you write again?

Your friend

Charlie

Fay of the Green Eyes
Breaksea Island, near
Albany, Western Australia

I had to hurry to write a reply. It was hard to know what to say. It might be the last letter before he goes into battle, so I just asked him to keep his head down and take care.

I am praying for his safe return and will send a longer letter with the next boat.

March 10th

Father heard there's been an outbreak of pneumonia amongst the troops. He also said four soldiers were killed trying to climb a pyramid. I hope one wasn't Charlie!

The southerly winds shrieked in the eaves at night, clamouring against the walls, trying to get inside. As the wind howled, Fay snuggled deeper under the bedcovers with her journal, reminding herself that it was only the wind.

March 17th

On nights like this, when Father is working and the wind takes on a haunting wail, I imagine the voices of the convicts who built the lighthouse. It must have been lonely for them in 1858. So far from home and family … Then, when the wind rattles the shutters and loosens the roof iron, tingles spook along my spine. I wonder how many of those poor souls died here.

April 21st

More postcards arrived today, all addressed to 'The Little Girl on Breaksea Island'. This one is my favourite.

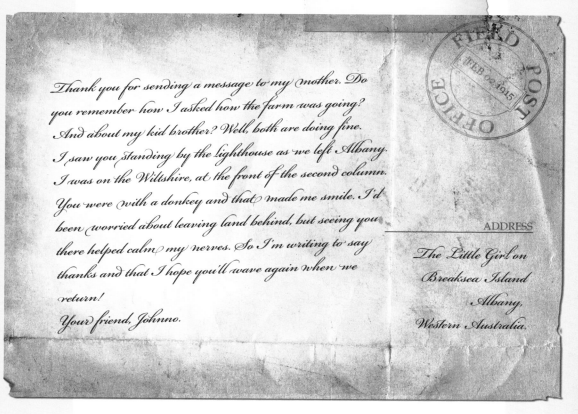

Thank you for sending a message to my mother. Do you remember how I asked how the farm was going? And about my kid brother? Well, both are doing fine. I saw you standing by the lighthouse as we left Albany. I was on the Wiltshire, at the front of the second column. You were with a donkey and that made me smile. I'd been worried about leaving land behind, but seeing you there helped calm my nerves. So I'm writing to say thanks and that I hope you'll wave again when we return!

Your friend, Johnno.

ADDRESS

The Little Girl on Breaksea Island Albany, Western Australia.

Another soldier to add to my prayers. I hope he and Charlie are okay.

After the Australian soldiers landed at Gallipoli, every edition of the *Albany Advertiser* carried an update from the Middle East. Fay pored over the news, waiting and wondering.

April 28th

The Albany Advertiser says, 'a big battle between the Allies and the Turks has commenced at the Dardanelles. Troops have been landed at Enos and at Salva, Gallipoli and Bulair.'

May 5th

Today they reported, 'a landing on both sides of the Dardanelles under excellent conditions.' The Turks have taken prisoners, but our boys are advancing. Father says they're describing Gallipoli as 'our young nation's baptism of fire'. He tried to explain what that means, but I'm still not sure.

We sail tomorrow, Green Eyes. I can't give
details, but I'll imagine you praying for me as
I run into battle.
Yours, Charlie

ADDRESS

Fay of the Green Eyes
Breaksea Island,
near Albany
Western Australia

May 15th

*The news from Gallipoli is bad. I'm worried for Charlie. I
wish letters didn't take so long. Maybe one day there'll be a
faster way to send messages …*

May 16th

*Huge waves lashed the island last night. Spray soaked our
roof. I hope we don't get salt in the rainwater tanks again.*

May 30th

*Yesterday Stan brought another card from Charlie, but it was
written before the landings at Gallipoli.*

*S*tan waved an envelope as he climbed onto the jetty.

'There's a letter from your Charlie!'

'He's not *my* Charlie,' Fay said, stuffing the letter into her pocket.

Stan laughed. 'Aren't you going to read it?'

Fay blushed. 'I will later,' she said, 'after we've taken the stores to the house.'

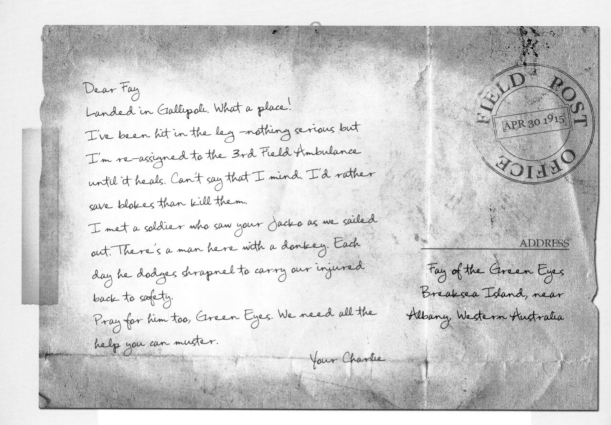

Dear Fay
Landed in Gallipoli. What a place!
I've been hit in the leg — nothing serious but
I'm re-assigned to the 3rd Field Ambulance
until it heals. Can't say that I mind. I'd rather
save blokes than kill them.
I met a soldier who saw your Jacko as we sailed
out. There's a man here with a donkey. Each
day he dodges shrapnel to carry our injured
back to safety.
Pray for him too, Green Eyes. We need all the
help you can muster.

Your Charlie

FIELD POST OFFICE
APR 30 1915

ADDRESS
Fay of the Green Eyes
Breaksea Island, near
Albany, Western Australia

June 14th

A letter from __my__ Charlie at last! I almost pushed Jacko up the hill so that I could read it in private.

It's bad luck about his wound, but he'll be safer working in the field hospital … I'd better stop writing, Father's calling for his morning tea.

—ANZAC COVE.—

Fay smiled at her father as she took the kettle off the hob.

'Everything all right?' he asked as she brewed a fresh pot of tea.

Fay nodded and passed him a thick slab of damper and jam.

June 16th

Before the troopships' visit everything was simpler. I was happy chatting to Jacko, Joe, Father and the birds. I didn't know I was lonely. But now that I have real friends to write to, everything has changed. I am restless. Breaksea feels too small. I want to see the world and go to the places on my postcards.

June 20th

I've written three letters to Charlie, one to Johnno and one to the donkey man at Gallipoli. Johnno wrote back but still no word from Charlie. And the news from Turkey keeps getting worse.

June 26th

Every evening the great-winged petrels return from fishing. They swirl and swoop with their long scythe-like wings spread wide, calling wik wik wik to their mates. Then, when the light has drained from the sky, they crash-land in their funny, clumsy way and stumble back to their nests. Their chorusing and cooing fills the night until just before dawn when they head back out to the continental shelf.

July 10th

The whales are back! It looks like being a busy season for the whalers. This year I'm keeping a record of them.

July 7 – one southern right near Michaelmas Island

July 9 – humpbacks – a mother and calf just off Breaksea

July 10 – pod of five or six humpbacks near Bald Head

July 12th

I hate the death-smell from the whaling station and now the shark packs have returned. Watching them patrol the deep channels makes me shiver.

Still no mail from Charlie. Why hasn't he written?

'Any letters?' Fay called as Stan stepped onto the jetty.

'Nothing for you, Fay, but there's one for your father. It's addressed to "The Lighthouse Keeper, Breaksea Island".'

Fay looked at the mark on the envelope.

'Why is there a letter from the war addressed to Father?' Fay asked. 'We don't have family serving overseas.'

Stan looked away as Fay steadied Jacko's load. She hurried him along the path.

'Father,' Fay called. 'Come quickly. There's a letter for you.'

Fay chewed her lip as she waited for him to open
the envelope. He scanned the page then looked up.
Before he could say anything, Fay ran.
She ran out of the cottage,
as far away from the
letter as she could.

Petrels screeched. The wind tore at Fay's hair. Waves crashed over the rocks below. She remembered the young men waving as they sailed off to war. She remembered the messages of love that she'd sent thousands of miles across Australia. She remembered the postcards addressed to 'The Little Girl on Breaksea Island' and the bottles that had washed up at Ellen Cove, each one sheltering a message of hope.

Fay crumpled onto the scratchy ground amongst the rabbit holes. How many letter writers would never return, she wondered as she curled into a ball and sobbed for the loss of a boy with hazel eyes and no loved ones.

Fay's eyes were rimmed with tears and windblown sand by the time Father found her.

'Charlie's commanding officer wrote that he died quickly,' Father said. 'He didn't suffer.'

'It's so unfair,' Fay cried.

'It is,' Father replied.

'I prayed for him …'

'I know.'

The lighthouse keeper stroked his daughter's hair. 'Come on now, dry your tears. Jacko is waiting by the cottage. He needs his dinner.'

'Charlie was my first real friend. Why did he have to die? And Mother? And Ada? It's not fair.'

Fay's father sighed. 'I don't know, Fay. Your mother would have said, "It's God's will," but really, I don't know …'

Fay leant against her father. She imagined Charlie crouching in a ditch, and rushing patients through the trenches to the safety of the field hospital. She could see him scribbling messages to her before dropping exhausted onto his blanket at the end of the day. Fay was sure she'd read a smile in the spaces between his words.

Had he thought of her before he died? Maybe in the end her friendship had made a difference. Maybe knowing there was someone at home thinking of him had helped Charlie to be brave.

The solitary eye of the lighthouse blinked across the dusk shadows. Its beam shone west, over the sea towards a bleak peninsula where hundreds of Turks and Australians still fought for a hillside drenched in blood.

Fay wiped her tears as the great-winged petrels soared home through the darkening sky.

About Fay

The idea for *Lighthouse Girl* was sparked by an article called 'The Long Goodbye' (*Weekend Australian*, 23 April 2005). Ron Critall wrote:

Perth man Don Watson tells of his mother, Fay Catherine Howe, daughter of the Breaksea Island lighthouse keeper. She was just 15 and stood on the island signalling to the departing fleet, almost certainly the last human contact with Australia. Numerous postcards came back to Albany from the Middle East, addressed to 'The little girl on Breaksea Island'.

Curious to find out more about Fay and her postcards, I tracked down Don Watson. He was enormously generous in sharing his family's story.

Although Fay's story is based on fact, some details I added in writing *Lighthouse Girl* are, by necessity, fictitious. The real Fay was the youngest daughter of Breaksea Island lighthouse keeper, Robert Wilkinson Howe. In 1912, Fay's sister, Ada, died just before her seventeenth birthday. Ada's infant child was left in the care of her mother, Hannah. Then in mid-1914, Fay's mother also died. Fay's elder siblings, Harold and Evelyn, lived away from Breaksea.

So in 1914, the 'little girl' of my story was actually working long hours looking after her father and the second lighthouse keeper, as well as caring for Ada's toddler. She wouldn't have had much time for daydreaming or sketching.

Conditions were harsh on Breaksea. The monthly supply boat was often unable to make the journey and Fay, who was an excellent shot, supplemented their meagre supplies with rabbit and mutton-bird stew.

Fay's Charlie is a fictitious character. The photograph on page 45 is of an Albany boy, Ned Wellstead, who was killed during World War One. Stan is also fictitious, though Albany resident Stan Austin did take supplies to Breaksea Island.

Jacko, the donkey, did live on the island and carried supplies up the steep, zig-zag track for many years.

The first contingent of Australian and New Zealand troops did mass in Albany Harbour for three days in October 1914 before sailing to the Middle East and cinematographers did film the departing fleet from Breaksea, though I'm not sure what Fay served them for dinner or whether she got to see the film at the Empire Theatre. Thirty-six troopships, escorted by six warships, carried 30,000 Australian and New Zealand men, along with medical staff and horses. Albany was the last sight of Australia many of the men ever had.

On 25 April 1930, after delivering a Requiem for the War Dead at 6am, Father Arthur White led a procession of parishioners to lay a wreath at Albany's War Memorial. They then climbed to the top of Mt Clarence overlooking Albany Harbour where Father White is reported to have said, 'As the sun riseth and goeth down, we will remember them.' This climb became an annual pilgrimage and is credited as the origin of the Anzac Day dawn service tradition.

You can find more photographs and information about
Breaksea Island on my website at:
www.diannewolfer.com

And teaching notes at: www.fremantlepress.com.au

Acknowledgements

Books take time to come to fruition and many people have helped bring *Lighthouse Girl* to publication. Firstly, I would like to thank the Department of Culture and the Arts, Western Australia. Their generous financial support gave me time to write a first draft and was deeply appreciated.

Thank you to the team at Fremantle Press, especially the unflappable Cate Sutherland, whose vision and willingness to experiment has given the book richness and layers; to Tracey Gibbs for her wonderful design work; to Brian Simmonds for capturing the wild beauty of Breaksea in his evocative charcoal illustrations; and to Ali Babington for modelling Fay.

I am grateful to the 'Breaksea Experts', Lawrence Cuthbert and maritime historian Adam Wolfe, for their ongoing help with practical and historical details. Accolades to the staff at Albany Public Library, especially the history buffs upstairs – Malcolm Trail, Sue Smith, Julia Mitchell and Dannielle Orr – who provide a valuable service to the community in preserving stories for future generations.

For archival photographs, thank you to the *Albany Advertiser*; Albany Public Library; Andrew Eyden, Colin Aspinall, Chris Roberts and Ian Lund from Albany Historical Society; staff at the Western Australian Museum Albany; descendants of William Brown; Lawrence Cuthbert; Bett Needle; Brian Malone and Don Watson. Thanks also to Edith Webb, and Eleanor and Sophie Cuthbert.

I am indebted to fellow writers in my critique group: Maree Dawes, Joy Kilian, Andrew Turk, Libby Corson, Barb Temperton, Emma Crook, Liane Shavian and also Tracey Lawrie and Peter Underwood. And my writing buddies in the Society of Children's Book Writers and Illustrators – especially Susanne Gervay for suggestions regarding fine-tuning the ending. Hugs to Sophie and other family members for listening to me obsess and for telling me when to stop.

And finally, an enormous thank you to Don and Peg Watson. From the beginning you trusted me with intimate family details and believed in the project. *Lighthouse Girl* is dedicated to you, Don, which is what I believe Fay would have wanted.

Picture Credits

Clippings from the *Albany Advertiser* recreated from microfilmed newspapers sourced via Albany Public Library History Collection; postcards from Charlie created using original period postcard designs; pages 4–5, world map (Zoomstudio istock.com), Prime Minister Cook (National Archives of Australia, 4746752); pages 8–9, Albany Brass Band (Albany Library History Collection, #0117), pages 12–13, sailing boat (Albany Library History Collection, #2706); pages 16–17, South Channel and Sugar Loaf Rock (courtesy descendants of William Brown); pages 20–21, donkey on jetty (Albany Historical Society P1997.485), Breaksea Island jetty (courtesy descendants of William Brown); pages 24–25, donkey (courtesy Bett Needle); pages 28–29, Queensland soldiers returning to their ship (Albany Historical Society); pages 32–33, Victorian troops marching through Albany (Western Australian Museum, Albany 161/142); pages 36–37, semaphore chart (garywg istock.com); pages 40–41, Albany soldiers (Albany Historical Society, top P1988.292, bottom P1988.329); pages 44–45, Private Edward Wellstead (Albany Historical Society P1990.20); pages 48–49, Howe family photographs (courtesy Willmott family, Busselton); pages 52–53, AIF fleet at anchor in King George Sound (Albany Historical Society); the departing fleet (from a painting by M. Dalton-Hall, image accessed via Western Australian Museum, Albany); pages 64–65, Madge Needle (courtesy Bett Needle); pages 68–69, troops in the Egyptian desert (Albany Historical Society P1988.335), Australian soldier with kangaroo mascot in front of the lines of the 9th and 10th Battalions at Mena Camp, Egypt (Australian War Memorial Negative Number C02588); pages 72–72, Christmas doily (author's own), South Channel at midnight (courtesy descendents of William Brown), Christmas card (courtesy Edith Webb); pages 76–77, postcards (author's own); pages 80–81, Empire Theatre (Albany Library History Collection, #2130); pages 84–85, Private Sydney Clunes (Australian War Memorial Negative Number P00346.001); pages 88–89, Driver Arthur Edward Attwell, at the foot of the Great Pyramid of Khufu (Australian War Memorial Negative Number J03261); pages 92–93, Breaksea Lighthouse (Albany Library History Collection, #2614); pages 96–97, 11th Battalion, 3rd Brigade, AIF on the Great Pyramid of Khufu (Australian War Memorial Negative Number P05717.001); pages 100–101, Anzac Cove (courtesy State Library of Western Australia, Battye Library 274022PD); page 118, Fay Howe (courtesy Don Watson).